This book should be returned to any branch of the
Lancashire County Library on or before the date shown

EBC

1 7 AUG 2017
1 3 JUN 2019

- 1 AUG 2019

2 6 AUG 2019

- 8 OCT 2019

2 9 FEB 2020

Lancashire County Library
Bowran Street
Preston PR1 2UX

Lancashire
County Council

www.lancashire.gov.uk/libraries

The Muddy Paws series

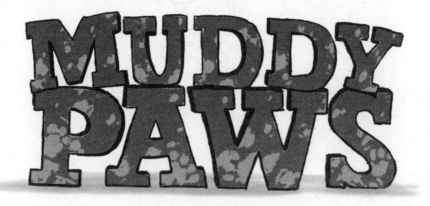

MUDDY PAWS

Rocking with Roxy and Rosie

JENNY OLDFIELD

Illustrated by Paul Howard

Hodder
Children's
Books

A division of Hachette Children's Books

First published in Great Britain in 2013
by Hodder Children's Books

A Catalogue record for this book is available
from the British Library

ISBN 978 1 444 91320 0

Printed and bound by CPI Group (UK) Ltd, Croydon, CR0 4YY

Hodder Children's Books
A division of Hachette Children's Books
Hachette UK Limited
338 Euston Road,
London NW1 3BH
www.hachette.co.uk

To Lola, Jude
and Evan –
my little stars!
JO

Chapter One

"Benji, this is Alfie. Alfie, meet Benji!" Lexi said with a broad smile.

Her little dog, Alfie, wagged his tail and said hello to Benji, a white, puppy-shaped bundle of running, jumping, yapping fun.

"This is the first time Benji has stayed away from home," his worried owner confessed.

"Don't worry – he'll be fine," Lexi's cousin, Lily, told the small, fair-haired boy. The two girls ran Muddy Paws in the grounds of Sea View Café, overlooking blue sea and sandy beaches. They both loved animals of every variety and especially furry little dogs like Benji. "He can live in Lexi's house with Alfie so he won't feel lonely."

"He might miss me while I'm away," sad six-year-old Oliver went on. "So I brought his favourite blanket and this toy." Handing over the ragged blanket and a chewed rubber bone to Lexi, Oliver gave a big sigh. "Here, Benji!" he called and the little terrier bounded up to him. "Be good – OK!"

Yipping and yapping, turning on the spot and bouncing up and down, little Benji didn't look at all sorry to say goodbye.

"Come on, Oliver." His mum stepped forward and took his hand. "It's time to go and catch the plane. Before you know it we'll be on holiday in Spain!"

Lily and Lexi picked up Benji and Alfie to

watch the visitors cross the Sea View lawn and get into their car. Oliver waved as the car set off down the lane and Lily waggled Benji's paw back at him.

"See you in two weeks!" Lexi called. "And don't worry about a thing!"

* * *

"So who's this little mischief-maker?" Lexi's dad, James, asked when Benji scooted ahead of Alfie into the kitchen at Sea View. James sat chatting with Lily's mum and dad, Jo and Matt.

Benji darted through the door and under the table. Straight away he snatched the edge of the red and white checked table cloth between his teeth and began to tug.

"Benji, stop that!" Lily cried as her dad's newspaper slid from the table and the puppy ignored her. He brought the cloth down on

top of himself and Alfie. All you could see under the cloth were two humped shapes wriggling to get free. "Hmm," she said.

Lexi grinned. "This is going to be interesting."

Together the girls lifted the cloth and peered down at the naughty visitor. "It looks like we'll be doing plenty of puppy training

with Benji," Lily decided.

The tiny terrier blinked then looked up at them with big, brown eyes. One white ear was pricked, the other flopped over his eye.

"Who can resist?" Matt laughed. "But girls, I'd say you're going to need all your Muddy Paws skills to teach this one some manners!"

It was the third week of August – more than halfway through the summer holidays – and Lily and Lexi's Muddy Paws animal agency was busier than ever.

"Let's type a list," Lily suggested early on Sunday afternoon.

"What of?" Lexi asked.

"Of pet problems solved by Muddy Paws so far." Happily Lily began to type:

June	July	August
4 guinea pigs	1 kitten	1 cat
1 school hamster	3 cats	2 dogs
1 rabbit	1 rabbit	1 puppy
	1 pony	
	1 puppy	

The list included Madcap, the cheeky Jack Russell terrier with the famous boy-band owner, and Breezy, the hard-to-handle foal at Dentwood Hall.

From hamsters to ponies and everything in-between – as the girls were forever reminding their clients, 'There's no problem too big or too small for us to solve."

And they'd done it all without any help from grown-ups, except when Lily's dad, Matt, had helped them set up the Muddy Paws website and printed their special logo on to white T-shirts. They'd also kept their promise to Lily's mum, Jo, and kept all animal visitors in the old stable at the bottom of the garden, well away from Sea View café and gift shop.

"But, Benji, you have to copy how Alfie behaves," Lily tried to tell their new visitor.

"Look and learn," Lexi agreed as they set

off later that afternoon for the beach. "Heel, Alfie!"

Straight away the little white and black dog came to heel.

"Heel, Benji!" Lily called.

Benji yapped and raced ahead of them along the cliff path.

"Hmm," Lily said again.

"Ouch!" Lexi cringed as Benji misjudged the bend and ran at top speed into a tangle of blackberry bushes. It took a while to pull him out and pick the thorns from his soft paws. "Maybe we should keep you on the lead until you know where you're going."

But no – Benji wanted to run. He squirmed and ducked out of reach, following Alfie to the wooden steps down on to the beach then overtaking him, almost falling head over heels to get to the beach first. By the time the girls and Alfie joined him, he was splashing in pools left by the outgoing tide, rolling in the sand and sprinting on to greet another dog walker and his brown and white terrier.

"Down, Benji!" Lexi yelled as she saw him jump up. "Whoops – that's . . ."

". . . Luke Walker!" Lily nodded. Luke had taken the place of Jude Wright as their favourite member of the boy band, Up Front. "He must be visiting his mum. C'mon – let's go!"

"Hi, girls!" By the time Lexi and Lily arrived, Luke was happily watching Madcap and Benji play at the water's edge while Alfie stayed obediently at Lexi's side.

"It's OK, you can play too," Lexi told him.

Soon all three dogs were chasing each other through the waves.

"We love your latest hit single – 'Lucky Us'," a breathless Lily told Luke. "We knew it would go straight to number one."

"Yeah, thanks," he murmured. But it seemed he didn't like to talk about his amazing boy band success and he soon turned the talk away from himself. "Anyway, how are things with you and Muddy Paws?"

"Cool," Lexi told him.

"More than cool," Lily added. "Actually excellent, thanks."

"The latest thing is that we have to find homes for three guinea pig babies." Lexi had a sudden thought and her brown eyes lit up. "Luke, I don't suppose you . . ."

"No!" He laughed and shook his head. "I'm not at home enough to look after one. And I don't think Mum would thank me for leaving her with an extra pet on her hands. Madcap's more than enough!"

"Oh well." Lexi knew they would have to think again.

"The babies are cute. They belong to the Simons twins," Lily explained. "At first Jon and Sam thought their guinea pig was a male and they called him Hubert, but it turns out *he* was a *she*. They had to call her Harriet instead and she had three babies."

"Funny," Luke grinned as they strolled along the beach together. "I'm sorry I can't help."

They chatted some more before Luke said goodbye and took Madcap home to Beech House.

Lexi and Lily sighed as they watched him go, letting Alfie and Benji play on in the water.

"He's gorgeous!" Lexi murmured.

"More gorgeous than Sammy, Jude and Ryan." Lily listed the other members of Up Front. "And we actually know him!"

"Lucky us!" Lexi giggled.

They walked with Alfie and Benji right to the far end of the beach, singing Up Front's latest number one as they went: " '*We're so lucky – lucky, lucky, lucky/ To be with you/ Knowing you'll be tru-u-ue . . .*' "

The waves lapped at their ankles, the sun shone down on them and life was good.

Chapter Two

When Lily and Lexi got back to Sea View, Jo was getting ready to go on a run. She was at the gate, dressed in running gear and trainers, clutching a water bottle. "Luke just dropped off two signed copies of Up Front's latest CD. He said he promised he'd give them to you way back in June," she told the girls. "I left them on the kitchen table."

"*We're so lucky – lucky, lucky, lucky!*" they trilled as they rushed into the house with Alfie and Benji, only to find they had unexpected visitors.

"Oops!" Lily blushed.

Her dad winked from behind the visitors' backs. "Girls, I'd like you to meet Charlie and Emma Golding. They live at Lane's End and they popped in to speak with someone from Muddy Paws."

"That's us!" Lexi exclaimed, pointing to the logo on the front of her T-shirt. "How can we help?"

"We're not sure that you can," Emma began. She was a small woman with mid-length wavy brown hair, wearing a blue patterned top and jeans.

"We have an unusual request," Charlie confirmed. Dressed in a faded black T-shirt and ragged jeans, he seemed surprised that Lily and Lexi ran Muddy Paws. "We looked at your website and thought you'd be older."

Lexi shrugged. She and Lily were only ten, so what could she say?

"We're very good with animals," Lily assured the visitors. "We can train puppies and teach older dogs to do agility courses. We know how to do horse whispering with ponies . . ."

". . . Cure cats from peeing on carpets," Lexi added proudly.

"That's very . . . hygienic." Emma paused until she found the right word and her nose wrinkled slightly. "What else?"

"We can train dogs to stop chewing shoes."

"Excellent," Charlie nodded.

"Down, Benji!" Lexi spoke sternly to Oliver's puppy as he jumped up at Emma.

The little rascal ignored her and went on jumping. Embarrassing, or what!

"What a little cutie!" Emma grinned. "Anyway, we're not asking you to look after another puppy."

"No, like I said – our request is unusual," Charlie insisted. "Do either of you girls know what we do down at Lane's End?"

Lily and Lexi shook their heads and

glanced at Matt for help.

"They run a smallholding," Matt explained.

The girls still looked puzzled.

"A smallholding is a very small-scale farm where people grow vegetables and fruit and keep different sorts of animals – hens, a few sheep, maybe a goat."

"No goat," Emma said quickly. "The point is – Charlie and I have to go away for a few days."

"To a family funeral," Charlie said. "We don't have a choice – it's something we have to do."

"Normally we wouldn't leave the animals. Of course it's the middle of the summer so the sheep can look after themselves while we're away."

Lily frowned at Lexi. This all seemed a bit

of a mystery. "Do you want us to feed your chickens?" she asked.

"Well yes, that would be very good if you could pop in and do that every now and then," Charlie agreed. "But that's not really why we're here." He paused again then hurried on. "Actually we'd like you to look after Roxy and Rosie."

"Roxy and Rosie?" Lexi and Lily echoed. Lexi thought of rabbits while Lily had a picture of two cute hamsters in a cage.

"Our rare-breed, Gloucester Old Spot piglets," Emma told them.

"Piglets!" the girls cried.

"They're three months old," Charlie went on. "And we'd have to bring them here because they're quite a handful."

"Piglets?" Matt repeated and he made a sucking noise through his teeth. "Ooh, I'm not sure Jo would agree to that."

"Why not?" Lexi cried. "We can easily look after piglets, can't we, Lily?"

"Easy-peasy." But Lily sounded less certain than Lexi.

"Just for a few days," Emma assured them. "We have to set off tomorrow morning and drive up to Yorkshire. The funeral's on Tuesday. We'll be back home late Wednesday."

"Gorgeous, chubby, pink piglets!" Lexi cooed.

"White actually – with black spots," Charlie told her.

"You'd have to talk to your mum when she comes back from her run," Matt reminded Lily, who nodded.

"Roxy and Rosie. Do they have cute curly-wurly tails?" Lexi wanted to know.

"Never mind that," practical Lily frowned. "What do they eat? – No, don't worry, I can Google it and find out."

"We'd tell you everything you need to know," Emma assured her. "And we'd give you a big bag of grain pellets to keep you going."

Charlie cleared his throat and backed towards the kitchen door while Benji took a good sniff at the frayed hems of his jeans. "Look, we'll leave you now and give you time to think about it."

"This is our number." Emma handed Lily a small white card with details about Lane's End printed on it.

"So if you could give us a call later this evening, we'd be grateful," Charlie said, making a quick exit before Benji went further than just sniffing.

"Pigs stink!" Jo pinched her nose with an expression of disgust.

"No they don't, Aunty Jo!" Lexi sprang to Roxy and Rosie's defence.

"Not if we muck out their sty twice a day," Lily said.

"What sty?" As far as Jo knew, there was no such thing at Sea View.

"We'll do what we usually do," Lily explained. "We'll use the old stable out in the back paddock."

"And we'll put up electric fencing to make an outside space for them to run around in," Lexi added.

"OK, but they're noisy," Jo pointed out. "I don't want them oinking and squealing and upsetting my café customers."

"They won't," Lexi promised. "Honestly,

Aunty Jo – they're only a few weeks old – they'll be dead cute."

"Hmm." Jo twitched her nose if she could already smell Roxy and Rosie. "I'm just not sure. What do you think, Matt?"

He tutted and made the sucking-teeth noise. "Maybe it would be OK. It's only for three days."

Please! Lexi and Lily surprised Benji and Alfie by holding hands and doing an impatient dance around the room.

"And they're titchy!" Lexi promised.

"We'd be able to take photos and put them on our Muddy Paws website," Lily pointed out. "It'd be really good publicity."

Please!

"You won't let them anywhere near the café?" Jo checked again.

She's starting to weaken. She's going to say yes!

Lexi and Lily held their breaths.

"Oh, OK – why not?" Jo sighed at last.

Yes! The girls jumped and hugged each other then they scooped up the dogs and hugged them too.

"Am I mad?" Jo asked Matt.

He laughed. "No. A naughty puppy and two little Gloucester Old Spot piglets – what can possibly go wrong?"

Chapter Three

"Here they are – Roxy and Rosie!" Charlie
Golding announced as he opened the back
door of his old Volvo estate.

It was early on Monday morning and Lexi
had said bye to her dad and cycled through
the village with Alfie and Benji running
beside her, arriving at Sea View just as the
Goldings pulled into the car park.

"It's a tight squeeze but they still fit into a
pet carrier – just!" Emma told Lily and Lexi.
"They're quite heavy so Charlie will lift
them out and carry them for you. Where

will they be staying?"

"In the old stable," Lily answered. "We've laid straw on the floor for a bed and we've put up an electric fence in the paddock."

"Perfect," Emma smiled. She and Charlie let the girls lead the way past the cottage and the café, into the field at the back.

"*Oink!*" said a little voice from inside the pet carrier.

"Aah, cute!" Lexi whispered to Lily.

A second small piglet snuffled and snorted as Charlie set the carrier down on the grass. "Shall I let them out?" he asked.

Lily carefully closed the gate then nodded. She'd already read up about piglets and was dying to see Roxy and Rosie in the flesh.

"Ready!" Charlie said. And he opened the door of the pet carrier.

Whoosh! Two white shapes hurtled out,

oinking and snorting. The piglets ran round and round in circles, kicking their little trotters out behind them, rolling in the grass, springing up and whirling around again.

"Wow!" Lexi and Lily sighed, while Alfie backed away towards the gate and Benji hid behind Lily's legs.

"The one with three spots on her back is Roxy," Emma explained. "And the one with just one big spot is Rosie."

The piglets hardly stopped still long enough for the girls to make out their markings. "Are they always this lively?" Lily asked.

"Oh no, they do sleep – sometimes," Charlie grinned. "And they slow down if you give them some food. Watch this." Drawing two apples from his jacket pocket, he squatted down and held them out.

"*Snort – snuffle – snort!*" Roxy and Rosie made a beeline for the treat.

And now Lily and Lexi could tell them apart – Roxy with three small black spots, Rosie with one big splodge on her bottom. Apart from that they looked exactly the same – two little white barrels with big floppy ears and sturdy legs, pink snouts and sharp, dainty trotters.

Crunch! The piglets snaffled the apples, gulped them down and came trotting towards Alfie and Benji.

Alfie cocked his head to one side. Benji stayed in hiding behind Lily until she picked him up, cuddled him and held him safe.

"What's wrong, Benji?" Lexi giggled. "Haven't you ever met a piglet before?"

"So we brought their grain pellets," Emma hurriedly told Lexi and Lily as she handed over a big bag of food. "You give each piglet one pound of solid food per month of age, which means three pounds per piglet per day, plus any vegetable scraps, fruit, cheese or yogurt you would otherwise throw away."

"Coolio. I'll ask Mum to save us scraps from the café," Lily beamed.

"*Oink!*" Roxy cried, butting her head hard against Charlie.

"That's the lot – I have no more apples," he told her, standing up quickly before she pushed him over.

Rosie wouldn't take no for an answer. She snuffled at his baggy jeans then reared up on her hind legs to sniff at his pocket.

"Ouch – sharp trotters!" he cried.

"They *are* so cute!" Lexi exclaimed. "Look, Lily – see how their big, floppy ears come right down over their beady little eyes!"

"Their tails aren't as curly as I expected," Lily said thoughtfully. "And they're a lot – well, fatter!"

"But you love them, don't you?" Lexi prompted.

Lily nodded. "Totally," she agreed.

* * *

"Piglets are so cute you just want to cuddle them!" Lexi told her dad when she and Lily called in at the house on their way to Lane's End.

It was lunch-time and Roxy and Rosie had settled down nicely in their Muddy Paws holiday home.

Emma and Charlie had said goodbye and driven off with a rattle and small pop of exhaust fumes. Lexi and Lily had put the piglets to bed in the old stable then checked the electric fence to make sure all the posts were firm and the electricity could be switched on later that afternoon when they let the visitors out in the run to play.

"Don't worry – we'll let you both out for some exercise when we get back from feeding the chickens," Lily had explained.

"*Oink, oink,*" the piglet twins had agreed. Then they'd scuffled at the straw with their trotters and settled down deep into their clean bed.

"Uncle James, you should see them – they're so cheeky!" Lily said.

"They're cuddly and cheeky and fat," Lexi grinned.

"And clever," Lily added.

The piglet visitors had already learned how to kick over their bucket and hoover up the grain pellets straight from the floor into their mouths – a much quicker way of getting at their feed than leaving it in the bucket. They'd also worked out that poor little Benji was scared stiff of them and more than once they'd decided to tease him by charging straight at him and making him leap up into Lily's arms.

"And you're sure you can cope?" Lexi's dad asked. "Did the Goldings leave contact

details, just in case you need to get in touch?"

Lily nodded. "Emma told us all about Gloucester Old Spots."

"And now you're going to tell me," James grinned, settling in for a long lecture.

"People used to keep them in their orchards," Lexi rushed on. "Old Spots ate windfall apples and foraged for food."

" 'Foraged' means they dug for roots and snuffled around the trees to find mushrooms in August and nuts in the autumn." Lily took over. "They're a rare breed. There are less than one thousand breeding females in the whole country."

"So we have to take extra special care of them."

"They like you to scratch behind their ears – it makes them really happy," Lily explained. "Mind you, we haven't got close enough to do that yet. Roxy and Rosie are like little kids – they play around all the time then they just run out of energy and fall asleep."

James had broken off from his work at the computer and he came out into the garden to see Lexi and Lily off. "Wouldn't you like to leave Alfie and Benji here for a while – let them have a little nap?" he asked.

"Good idea," the girls agreed.

* * *

So Lexi's dad took the little dogs inside the house while Lily and Lexi cycled half a mile down a quiet lane until they came to the Goldings' quaint smallholding.

"This is it," Lexi announced as she read the sign on the gate.

They got off their bikes and propped them against the fence. Lane's End was the prettiest house the girls had ever seen. It had a thatched roof and white walls with a bright blue front door. The garden was full of red rose bushes, with honeysuckle climbing over the porch. Around the back of the house the girls found a neatly laid out vegetable plot with peas and beans, carrots, onions and lettuces all planted in straight rows. Behind that there was a yard with a wire fence where Emma and Charlie kept hens. Beside it was an empty field with a pig sty and beyond that another field with a dozen sheep.

"Wow, now I know what I'm going to do when I grow up!" Lexi cried as she and Lily trod the narrow path down to the fenced yard. There were six hens – three brown, one white and two black-and-white speckled – pecking at the dust. "I'm going to be a smallholdinger!"

"Smallholder," Lily said quietly, studying the hen house that Emma and Charlie had built. It was about the size of a large kennel, raised from the ground on a stone platform and made out of straight tree branches, like a mini log cabin.

The hens pecked, strutted and bobbed in

their yard, puffing out their chests then squatting in the dirt and spreading their wings to take a dust bath.

"Problem." Lexi frowned as she and Lily stood outside the wire compound. "Where did Emma say they kept the hen food?"

"She didn't," Lily said. Then she pulled out the phone where she'd stored the Goldings' number. "I'll call her and find out."

It was Charlie who answered. "Hi, girls. Are you having trouble with R and R?"

"No, Roxy and Rosie are fast asleep. They're fine, thanks. We're at Lane's End, wondering where you keep the food for the chickens."

"Oh, sorry, we didn't explain. It's in the shed next to the veg patch."

"I'll find it." Lily went to look. She opened

the shed door and peered inside.

"The poultry food is on the top shelf," Charlie told her. "Plus you can pick a lettuce and feed it to the hens. They'll like that."

"Great, thanks." Lily was about to end the call but Charlie remembered something else.

"There's another thing we forgot to mention – about the piglets."

"Go ahead," Lily said as she went into the shed and reached for the bag of hen food.

"Roxy and Rosie are music fans," Charlie explained. "They have favourite songs which we put on a CD to keep them entertained while we muck them out. You'll find it on the shelf to the left of the shed door."

"No way!" It took Lily a while to take in what Charlie had just told her.

"Believe me," he laughed. "I'm not kidding."

Lily made a surprised face at Lexi as she came out of the shed. "What kind of music do the piglets like?"

Lexi's eyebrows shot up and she stared back at Lily.

"Anything," he replied. "Pop, opera, rap. But their favourite style of music is heavy metal – the louder and more head-bangier the better."

Chapter Four

"Loud?" Lexi asked.

"And head-bangy," Lily insisted.

They'd cycled back to Sea View cottage after feeding the Goldings' chickens and were looking for Jo's old CD player in the cupboard under the stairs.

Matt heard the sounds of the contents of the cupboard being emptied into the hallway and came downstairs. "What's up?" he asked.

"Dad, have you heard of heavy metal?" Lily wanted to know. "What kind of music is it?"

"Besides being loud and head-bangy?" Lexi added.

"Heavy metal?" Matt stumbled over a pair of Lily's old wellies. "That would be Led Zeppelin and Black Sabbath, Iron Maiden and Judas Priest – all the old bands. Why?"

"'Cos Roxy and Rosie love it," Lexi told him. "We're going to play it to them when they wake up."

"Whoa!" Matt said as he shook his head. "It's not exactly cheerful, whistle-while-you-work music, let me tell you. It's usually about war and dying, among other things. And it's very, very loud."

Lily and Lexi grinned. "We don't care. The piglets like it," they declared.

* * *

Boom-boom-boom! The drum rolls almost burst Lily and Lexi's eardrums and sent Alfie and

Benji sprinting inside the cottage for cover. Guitars whined and a bass beat pounded out across Sea View's lawn.

Roxy and Rosie woke up from their afternoon nap. Their snouts began to twitch and they raised themselves from their straw bed.

"Here, pig, pig, pig!" Lily called as she stood in the paddock and rattled a bucket of pellets. But her voice was drowned by the heavy metal roar.

Lexi stood ready with a too-big pair of yellow rubber gloves, a mucking-out fork and a shovel. "Louder!" she yelled.

Boom-boom-boom! Whine-twang-whine!

"Lily, Lexi, what on earth is that racket?" Jo demanded, striding out of the gift shop and across the lawn. When she reached the gate into the field she stopped and stared.

11

"Here, pig, pig, pig!" Lily rattled and called.

Inside the old stable, Roxy and Rosie slowly yawned and stood up. Their heads started to nod to the mad, head-banging beat.

"What the . . . ?" Matt asked as he joined Jo at the gate.

Lexi peered into the stable. She saw the piglets nod their heads and wiggle their backsides in time to the music. "Wow!" she said.

"Here, pigs!" Lily called.

And out they came, little trotters raised, stomping into the field. Roxy and Rosie held their heads and flapped their ears to and fro. They shimmied and shook from snout to tail.

"It's true – they actually *like* it!" Matt murmured.

"See!" Lexi called.

Lily rattled the pellets and watched the piglets stomp towards her. "It works!" she yelled at Lexi. "Now you grab the chance to go in there and muck out the mess while I keep them happy out here."

* * *

Lexi and Lily wrote on the Muddy Paws website.

Rocking with Roxy and Rosie
Guess what – our Gloucester Old Spot
piglets love heavy metal music
– *so-o-o* cute!

It was Tuesday morning and the girls had a busy day ahead. Lexi typed:

We've already found two homes for Harriet's babies. Our teacher, Mrs Taylor, has decided to adopt Georgie and Lucy went to a good home in Mellingham. If there's anyone out there reading this who wants the last, lovely little guinea pig for a pet, just leave a comment and we'll get in touch.

"Girls, you smell a bit whiffy," Jo commented as she came into the kitchen for more milk for the café. "Have you been working with the piglets?"

Lily bent her head and sniffed her Muddy Paws T-shirt. She wrinkled her nose. "Mum's right," she told Lexi.

"We were out in the paddock making sure the electric fence worked. Roxy let Lily stroke her," Lexi explained to her aunt. "And I got a cuddle from Rosie."

"That's explains the pong," Jo said, exiting with the milk.

"Clean T-shirts?" Matt suggested from his place at the kitchen table, where he was busy making parcels of special tea which he sent out to customers.

"We've just got time to change before Will Jonson arrives with his lop-eared rabbit," Lily said. "He wants to know why Robbie has a runny nose."

"Then we'll give Benji his first lesson in learning to sit and stay," Lexi decided. "That'll take about half an hour."

Lily looked at her watch. "Then it'll be lunch-time."

"Then time to go back to Lane's End to feed the hens."

"Then back here to muck out the piglets."

"Or we could do that first – before we change our T-shirts," Lexi suggested with a twinkle in her eye. "We can leave Benji's lesson until this afternoon."

"Coolio!" Lily was quick to agree as Will arrived with his black rabbit cosily snuggled on a cushion inside a pet carrier.

Both girls agreed – the more time they got to spend with adorable Roxy and Rosie the better.

* * *

"I think Robbie might just be too hot," Lexi told Will Jonson after she and Lily had taken a look at his rabbit and they'd checked his symptoms online.

"Rabbits get runny noses if you keep them out in the sunshine without any shade. Or else, if he lives inside, maybe you're keeping him too close to a radiator."

Will thought about it. He went to the same school as Lily and Lexi and that was how he'd got to know about Muddy Paws. "Don't

rabbits like the sun?" he asked.

"Yes, but not too much. They have to
have somewhere cooler that's in the shade."

"Try making him a little shelter," Lily
suggested. "And if that doesn't stop his nose
running, you have to take him to the vet."

"OK." Will nodded and carefully put
silky, shiny Robbie back into the carrier.
Suddenly he wrinkled his nose and seemed

to be in a hurry to leave. "Thanks. See you!" he called as he hurried out.

Still working at the table, Matt sniffed loudly. "Whiffy!" he reminded them. "However much you two love those little piggies, they definitely do pong, believe me!"

But it didn't put Lexi and Lily off. They just grinned and ran outside with the CD player and the heavy metal CD.

Bang-boom-bang! To the sound of crashing drums and whining guitars, they lured Roxy and Rosie out of the old stable and let them rootle and run, wriggle and stomp their little trotters in the lush green grass.

* * *

"Watch this, Alfie! Benji, come and take a look!" Lily and Lexi decided that after lunch was a good time for the two little dogs to make friends with Roxy and Rosie so they took them out to the run where the piglets roamed.

"Stay here by the gate," Lexi told Alfie. "No, don't run away. Show Benji what a big, grown-up boy you are."

Alfie settled by her side, his head resting on his front paws. He peered warily under the gate at the strange, smelly white creatures.

"Stay, Benji – that's a good dog." Lily crouched down beside him and stroked him gently. "See – there's nothing to be scared of."

Benji quivered. It was clear he didn't believe her.

"Here, pigs!" Lexi called, stepping on to the bottom rung of the gate and offering Roxy and Rosie two nice juicy carrots.

Food! The piglets spotted the carrots and charged down the run. They flung themselves at the gate, poked their snouts between the bars and sent Lexi crashing sideways against the metal latch. The latch sprang up and the gate swung open.

Freedom! Roxy and Rosie saw the smooth, open lawn, the fish pond and the open café door. In a flash they left the field and sprinted like greyhounds across the lawn.

Alfie whined and looked up at Lexi. *What now?*

Benji slunk between Lily's legs and almost tripped her as she helplessly watched the runaway piglets.

"Roxy, Rosie – come back here!" Lily cried.

But they'd smelled freshly baked cake and nothing would stop them as they raced for the café door.

"Alfie, fetch!" Lexi said.

Lily grabbed Benji and closed her eyes. If the piglets got into the café her mum would never forgive her. She pictured sharp trotters slipping and sliding over the tiled floor, she heard the oinks and squeals that the pair would make as they sank their chops into the nearest lemon drizzle cake or Victoria sponge. "No!" she groaned.

"Fetch!" Lexi said again.

This time Alfie obeyed. He darted straight as an arrow across the lawn and took one giant leap clean over the small fish pond. He raced on and got to the café door ahead of the greedy piglets.

"Good Lord!" an elderly café customer cried as he spotted what was happening outside on the lawn. "Did you know you had pigs in your garden?"

It brought Jo running to the door.

"Please, no!" Lily whispered to herself, realizing there was only one thing that she could possibly do. She picked up the two carrots that Lexi had dropped.

Grrr! Alfie crouched low in the doorway and bared his teeth. The fur at the back of his neck stood on end.

Roxy and Rosie saw him and screeched to a halt on the gravel pathway. They didn't

like the look of those pointed, sharp teeth so
they veered off to one side, back on to the
lawn.

"Here, pigs!" Lily called. She stood in the
paddock and held up the carrots. "Here,
Roxy! Here, Rosie!"

More food! Not as good as lemon drizzle
cake, but better than nothing. The piglets
took one last lingering look at the café door

and saw guard dog Alfie still blocking their way. They turned their snouts towards Lily and the juicy carrots.

Carrots will have to do, they thought. And they flapped their ears and wiggled their spotted backsides as they trotted back across the lawn and in through the gate.

Chapter Five

It was Tuesday evening and all was peaceful at Sea View.

"Everything OK out there?" Jo called as she closed the café and gift shop for the day and headed back to the cottage.

Lily and Lexi leaned on the paddock gate, watching Roxy and Rosie tuck into a big bowl of vegetable scraps.

"Everything's cool," Lily told her.

"Good. Don't go far – dinner will be ready in an hour," her mum reminded the girls from the kitchen doorway.

"So is it OK if we nip over to Lane's End to check on the chickens?" Lexi asked. "We've got time – honest."

"Fine," Jo agreed. "It's home-made lasagne so I can keep it in the oven for you if you get held up."

"Yum." Lily was already hungry and she liked the sound of lasagne. Still, it was hard to tear herself away from Roxy and Rosie happily snorting and munching their way through a pile of cabbage leaves and apple peel.

"Just time for a quick stroke?" Lexi suggested. Without waiting for an answer, she climbed over the wooden gate and jogged over to Rosie, who happened to have her back turned and her snout deep in the bowl. "Who's a pretty piggie!" she cooed as she drew near.

Whack! Rosie kicked out with her back legs and landed her trotters against Lexi's shins.

"Ouch!" Lexi fell forward and rolled in the grass.

Lily too climbed the gate and made straight for Roxy, making sure not to come up from behind. "Here, pretty pig!" she called. "Who'd like a lovely scratchy- scratch behind her floppy ears?"

Roxy looked up. She had half a cabbage leaf hanging from her mouth and a warning look in her small round eyes that said, *Don't bother me – I'm busy eating!*

Lily frowned and hung back. She watched Lexi pick herself up. "Yuck!"

"Yuck – what?" Lexi's legs were still hurting from Rosie's sharp kick.

"Your T-shirt," Lily pointed out. "It looks like you rolled in . . ."

"Pig poo!" Lexi sighed as she twisted round and studied the brown marks all down her back. "Oh well, who cares?"

Lily's mouth twitched then she broke into a wide grin. Meanwhile, Roxy and Rosie munched on.

"Laugh as much as you like," Lexi muttered. Deciding to leave the piglets to

their supper, she climbed back over the gate, ready to grab her bike and cycle to Lane's End. "Real smallholdingers don't care how bad they smell – they just ignore it and get on with their work!"

* * *

By the time Lily and Lexi had cycled down the lane to the Goldings' farm, the golden sun was sinking low in the sky and the chickens had already gone into their coop to roost. The sheep in the far field were still quietly grazing, and beyond that the girls could see the sea sparkling in the evening light.

"Let's take a quick peek inside the hen-house," Lily suggested.

Lexi agreed. She went up to the coop, crouched down and peered in through the door. " . . . Four-five-six," she counted.

With their chest feathers puffed out and heads drooping sleepily, the Goldings' chickens were all present and correct.

"Cool," Lily nodded. The hens looked cosy and comfy on their perches and she thought how nice it would be to keep a few chickens at Sea View. Leaving the yard and carefully closing the gate behind them, she shared her latest idea with Lexi.

"First, they're easy-peasy to look after," she began. "You just have to make sure they have grain and water."

"Plus a few lettuce leaves," Lexi added.

"They could be free range."

"But you'd need a wire-netting fence to keep foxes out."

"Mum would get lots of fresh eggs for the café."

"Yeah, that'd be cool."

By the time the girls had cycled up the lane and on to the main street through the village, Lily had definitely decided that she was going to keep hens. "Just three or four," she told Lexi. "I'll persuade Mum and Dad that they won't be any trouble. Everything will be easy-easy-peasy."

Sea View was in sight and it was Lexi's turn to grin at her cousin. "Yeah, whatever!" she laughed as she cycled across the small car park and propped her bike against the garage wall.

"Why not? Loads of people do it!" Lily insisted.

Lexi knew that her busy Uncle Matt and Aunty Jo might well say no to chickens. "Dream on," she murmured.

"I will," Lily replied stubbornly, following

her cousin into the cottage. Without dreams, what was life anyway?

* * *

HOW'S ROBBIE? As soon as she'd finished dinner, Lexi texted Will Jonson.

BETTER, he texted back. WE BUILT HIM A SHELTER.

THAT'S GREAT ☺, Lexi sent a final message. "Will says Robbie's runny nose is cured," she told Lily.

"Hmm." Lily was deep in thought. The family talk about keeping hens hadn't gone as well as she'd hoped.

"Maybe not right now," her dad had told her when she brought up the subject between mouthfuls of lasagne.

"B-b-but . . . they'd lay fresh eggs," she'd protested.

"Your dad's right – Muddy Paws already

takes up a lot of your time," Jo had agreed.

"B-b-but . . ." It had been no good – the hen question had got a big fat no.

"Lily, did you hear what I said?" Lexi asked as they washed the dinner pots at the kitchen sink. "Robbie the rabbit is better."

"OK, cool," Lily sighed. She finished the dishes and wiped her hands dry, then she took a dog lead from the hook on the back of the door. "C'mon, Benji – walkies!"

The little white pup crawled out from under the table and yipped. He jumped up and whirled in the air, landed and did a small excitement wee on the floor.

"Paper towel," Lexi offered helpfully.

Together they wiped up the puddle and Lexi and Alfie joined Lily and Benji on the evening walk.

"Where are we going?" Lexi asked Lily as Alfie stayed quietly to heel.

Benji pulled and strained at the lead.

"Along the cliff path as usual?" Lily suggested. The sun was setting and the sky was pink – there wouldn't be time to walk all the way to the beach.

"Are you OK?" Lexi checked with Lily as they trod the narrow path. To one side there were tall fuchsia bushes and brambles, to the other a steep drop down towards the cliffs and the beach. "Are you still sad about the hens?"

Lily nodded. "But Dad did say 'not right

now'. That's not actually 'no', is it?"

"I guess." Lexi walked ahead with Alfie, letting Lily and Benji follow. She could see Lighthouse Cottages to their right and beyond that the grounds of Dentwood Hall and the grand house overlooking the sea. "By the way, did we hear from Emma and Charlie about what time they'll be home tomorrow?"

Lily checked her phone. "No message," she replied.

Pausing to let Alfie sniff at an interesting tuft of grass, Lexi spotted ten-year-old Harry Finch waving at them from the grounds of the Hall. She waved back.

He shouted something which she couldn't hear.

She cupped her hands around her mouth. "What's up, Harry?" she yelled back.

He shouted again and ran to meet them.

"Did he say 'piglets'?" Lexi asked Lily, feeling her stomach tighten.

Suddenly Lily was paying attention. "'Piglets'?" she echoed.

Harry burst through the garden gate on to the path ahead of them. Molly, his golden retriever, came with him. "Have you got two piglets at Muddy Paws?" he demanded.

Lily and Lexi's hearts were in their mouths as they nodded.

"Well not any more, you haven't," Harry announced. He turned back into his garden and told them to follow. "Come and look at this."

Lexi, Lily, Alfie and Benji entered the grounds of Dentwood Hall. They saw beautiful beech trees and clipped hedges, a big lake, a stable yard and the house itself.

"Over there!" Harry told them.

They spotted three Dentwood Hall peacocks sprinting out of the bushes and across the lawn – one brilliant blue male and two brown peahens – long necks stretched out, small heads bobbing.

"*E-e-elp!*" They screeched the strange peacock cry.

And hot on their long tails came two white piglets with black spots on their backs, oinking and snorting, galloping over the Finches' perfect lawn.

"Are they yours?" Harry demanded, hands on hips.

Lexi and Lily groaned. "Yes," they admitted.

The peacocks ran for more cover. Roxy and Rosie trundled after them.

"*E-e-e-elp!*" the peacocks cried, diving

under some holly bushes.

"*Oink! Oink!*" The piglets threw themselves
headlong after them.

Chapter Six

"Ouch!" Lily cried. Holly bushes were prickly and Rosie was stuck right in the middle of one.

"Hey, this hurts!" Lexi yelped. Like Lily, she was belly-down and halfway under a holly bush, trying to grab hold of Roxy.

Harry, Molly, Alfie and Benji stood back and watched.

"Where did the peacocks go?" Lily asked Harry. All she could see ahead of her were twisted branches and prickly leaves.

"They ran right through the bushes and

out the other side," he told her. "It's only the piglets that got stuck."

Roxy and Rosie wriggled and squirmed. The more they struggled, the worse it got.

"Stay still," Lily pleaded with Rosie. She had one hand tucked under the piglet's fat tummy.

"*Oink-oink!*" poor Rosie squealed.

"You've got to let me help you," Lexi told Roxy. "If you stop struggling we'll soon get you out."

"*Oink!*" Roxy said faintly. She let Lexi get hold of her back legs and start to pull gently.

"That's right," Lexi murmured as she eased Roxy out from under the bush.

Lily too had managed to pull Rosie towards her. Soon all four emerged, covered in holly leaves and smarting from the sharp prickles.

"Rather you than me," Harry told the girls, trying to keep a straight face as they kept firm hold of the piglets and stood up. Holly leaves were tangled in their hair and their faces were streaked with dirt.

"Harry, we're really sorry," Lily began. "We've no idea how these two managed to escape."

"And thanks," Lexi added. She clutched Roxy's hot, fat little body close to her chest and let the piglet snuffle at her face with her broad, soft snout. "Hey, that tickles!"

"Yeah, thanks," Lily agreed. Without Harry's warning, who knew where Roxy and Rosie would have ended up?

Harry nodded and Molly wagged her tail. They went with the girls to the gate and watched them set off along the cliff path. "I guess this is the last time you'll be looking after piglets at Muddy Paws?" he called after them.

"No way!" Lexi replied quickly.

"Roxy and Rosie can visit any time they like!" Lily agreed as they marched on towards Sea View.

Because, no matter how much trouble the Golding piglets were turning out to be, Lexi and Lily had decided that the Gloucester Old Spots were still the cutest, cuddliest, cleverest animals around.

* * *

"This is where they dug their way to freedom," Lily decided as she and Lexi searched the pig run in the dying light.

Roxy and Rosie were safe inside the stable, sound asleep after their adventure, and now the girls were eager to work out where it had all gone wrong.

Lily pointed to a patch of bare earth next to one of the plastic posts they'd erected for the electric fence. A closer look told them that the piglets had used their trotters to scrape a hole deep enough for them to creep under the wire.

"But how did they get out on to the path?" Lexi wondered. It was obvious now how Roxy and Roxie had escaped from their run, but how had they got through the thick hedge that bordered the field?

The girls strode across the paddock to carry on their search.

"Here!" Lily pointed again. "See where rabbits have made a warren? The soil is soft and sandy so Roxy and Rosie could easily dig another hole. This is where they got out."

Lexi agreed. "So what we have to do

before we let them out of the stable tomorrow morning is put a better wire fence around the run," she decided. "More electric tape – closer to the ground, so they can't creep underneath."

"Good thinking." Lily knew it was time for them to head back to the cottage so she led the way. "Hear that?" she murmured as they passed the stable. The sun had finally sunk and a full moon had begun to shine. "That's the perfect sound of Rosie and Roxy snoring!"

* * *

"Are you sure the electric current is turned off?" a worried Matt asked Lily and Lexi next morning.

"Definitely, one hundred per cent." Lexi had cycled over from her house to Sea View before breakfast, eager to help Lily with the work on the fence, and now she assured him that she'd flicked the switch inside the stable.

Lily was busy stretching tape between the slim white posts, placing it so close to the ground that Roxy and Rosie couldn't even poke their snouts under it.

"What about the music – it's not too loud?" Matt asked anxiously. This was what had brought him out of the cottage in the first place – the sound of heavy metal blaring out from the old stable.

"The piglets like it loud," Lexi explained. She pointed to the open door where Roxy and Rosie could be seen, happily shaking and shimmying. "Rock on, Roxy! Rock on, Rosie!"

"Maybe *they* do, but what about the neighbours?" her uncle asked.

Lexi shrugged then grinned. She began to

thrash her arms about and sing along. "*'There's trouble in your smile / Bad girl, don't you do me no wrong . . . duh, duh!'*"

"Whoa, steady on!" Matt pleaded, putting his hands over his ears and retreating back into the house. He shut the door on the whining guitars and throbbing drums.

Lily went on working, the piglets went on shimmying and Lexi thrashed and closed her eyes. When she next opened them, she found Harry standing there with Molly, staring open-mouthed.

"Oops!" Lexi giggled.

Harry swallowed hard. "I was taking Molly for a walk and decided to come this way to find out how the piglets were doing," he stammered.

"Duh-dah – see for yourself!" Lexi stood to one side to let Harry see the stomping piglets. "By the way, I forgot to ask you last night – how's Breezy?"

Breezy was the nervous foal belonging to Harry's mum, Rosemary. Lexi and Lily had worked hard earlier in the summer to build Breezy's confidence.

"She's great," Harry answered, his gaze

still glued to the piglets.

" *'Bad girl, don't you do me no wrong!'* " The lead singer screamed out the lyrics while the piglets nodded their heads and waggled their bums in time to the beat.

"Right – I'd best be going," Harry decided hastily. This was too weird for him so he and Molly turned and walked away as fast as they could.

Then Jo came out of the café carrying a dish of yogurt and two wrinkled apples. "Can't you turn the music down?" she complained to Lily, who had left off working on the fence.

"OK – I suppose Roxy and Rosie have done enough head-banging for now." It was Lexi who ran across to the stable to lower the volume.

Jo pursed her lips. "Lily, are you sure you

and Lexi can handle this situation?" she asked anxiously. "After all, Charlie and Emma aren't due back until later today. How can we be sure the piglets won't try to escape again?"

"Don't worry – we've made the fence better," Lily assured her. "Anyway, if we give the piglets loads of apples and other treats, they won't need to go foraging."

"That's right, Aunty Jo." Lexi came back and helped Lily stick up for the piglets. "It wasn't their fault they went walkabout yesterday. We just didn't give them enough food."

"Anyway, Mum, helping Emma and Charlie to look after Roxy and Rosie is really, really important." Lily gazed proudly at the playful little Old Spots as they trotted out of the stable and began to roll and wriggle in the grass. "Remember they're on the list of endangered species."

"Yeah, they're a very rare breed," Lexi agreed. "Lily and me – we're doing our bit for animal conserving."

"Conserv*ation*," Lily said. "Honestly, Mum – they'll be fine at Muddy Paws from now on."

Jo sighed. "I suppose it's only until the end of the day."

"That's right!" Lexi cried. "Only a few more hours."

"We'll look after them," Lily promised. "We'll bring our breakfasts out here and then have a picnic lunch. We won't take our eyes off them."

"Not for a single minute," Lexi vowed.

Jo nodded and handed over the bowl of yogurt and the apples. "Fingers crossed," she told the girls, backing off as Roxy and Rosie smelled the treats and charged. She nipped quickly out of the paddock and let Lily slam the gate shut. "I don't usually like to look on the dark side, but today I'd say you're definitely going to need all the luck you can get!"

Chapter Seven

"You watch the piglets while I make some phone calls," Lexi told Lily after an open-air breakfast of Cheerios followed by Nutella on toast.

She left Lily using a long stick to scratch Roxy behind the ears while Rosie nosed around the stable door in search of dandelion leaves.

"Not so sunny today, huh?" her Uncle Matt called across the yard as he set off for the post office on his bike. A damp mist had rolled in off the sea during the night and the morning was chilly.

Lexi didn't care about the weather – she had work to do.

"Hi, Harry," she said over the phone to their friend from Dentwood Hall. "You left Muddy Paws a text message for us to call you. What was it about?"

"Guinea pigs," Harry told her. "Dominic Harris goes to my school in Mellingham – he says wants to adopt one of Harriet's babies."

"Excellent!" Jotting down Dominic's name and number, Lexi explained that the one baby left was male. "He's called Eric," she explained. "Is that what Dominic would like?"

"Put his name down for now," Harry decided. "I'll talk to Dominic and call you back."

Coolio! Lexi was so pleased after she finished her chat with Harry that she logged on to the Muddy Paws website. "SUCCESS!" she typed. "WE THINK WE FOUND A HOME FOR OUR LAST GUINEA PIG BABY!"

And while I'm at it, I may as well text Luke and tell him thanks for the CDs, she decided, humming the tune to 'Lucky Us' as she worked.

Then she went back and read a new e-mail from a lady in the village who had lost her four month old grey kitten. June Amos asked:

CAN YOU HELP ME FIND HIM, PLEASE? I CAN SEND YOU A PHOTO OF CASPAR. PERHAPS YOU COULD PUT IT ON YOUR WEBSITE?

Lexi wrote back to say that Muddy Paws would be glad to help.

After this, it was time to go and see how Lily was getting on in the paddock.

She took Alfie and Benji with her through the swirling mist. They found Lily wearing the yellow rubber gloves, playing loud music and busily clearing out the piglets' dirty bedding. Meanwhile, Roxy and Rosie were in the run, tucking into a bucket of feed pellets.

" '*We're gonna fight in the streets tonight!*' " Lily yelled along to the lyrics. " '*Duh-duh-duh . . . Shoot out the light!*' "

Alfie and Benji whined but Lexi grinned and joined in the head-banging chorus. " '*Shoot out the light! Shoot out the light!*' " When she could see that Lily had finished mucking out, she went into the paddock with the dogs.

Roxy and Rosie heard them and came trotting quickly towards them, looking for food.

"I haven't got anything for you!" Lexi

giggled as she showed them her empty hands.

Alfie cocked his head then took a small step towards Roxy. He wagged his tail.

"Look – Alfie wants to make friends," Lexi explained.

Roxy stood still and let Alfie take another step, then another. Then – *"oink!"* – she lowered her head and charged.

"Oops!" Lily laughed as both Alfie and Benji tucked their tails between their legs and skedaddled.

"I was thinking – how about a quick visit to Lane's End?" Lexi said after she and Lily had stood a while watching Roxy and Rosie munching and nodding their heads in time to "Shoot Out the Light"! "These two will be OK by themselves for a few minutes."

"Hmm." Lily wasn't sure.

"They will – look, they still have plenty of pellets. And we'll leave the stable door open in case they want to go inside and take a nap."

"Hmm." Still Lily hesitated.

"H-e-n-s!" Lexi spelled out the magic word. "Lovely, feathery, clucking hens!"

Lily pictured the six gorgeous chickens strutting across the yard at Lane's End. "Oh OK then," she agreed.

"Wait here while I turn off the music!" Lexi scooted into the stable and flicked a switch. Then she rejoined Lily by the paddock gate.

"But not for long," Lily insisted, glancing over her shoulder at Roxy and Rosie. "Just for a few minutes – OK!"

* * *

It was still misty and there was a chill wind

coming off the sea when the girls arrived at Lane's End.

"Brrr – even the hens look cold!" Lexi said.

Today they didn't puff out their feathers and settle down for a cooling dust bath. Instead they stalked briskly across the yard, pecking in the dirt for corn husks and insects.

"Let's feed them and get back to Sea View." Lily still felt bad about leaving Roxy and Rosie. She went quickly to the garden shed and brought back a dish of small pellets. She scattered them across the yard and watched the hens rush to gobble them up. Then she closed the yard gate, ready to set off for home.

"Wait for me," Lexi told her as she strapped on her cycling helmet. Lily was already astride her bike and starting to pedal.

"Catch me up!" Lily called. *We should never have left Roxy and Rosie*, she thought. *That was a big mistake!*

They cycled hard up the lane and through the village, reaching Sea View just as four customers went into the gift shop. Jo saw the girls through the open door and gave them a wave.

Lily didn't wave back – she was too worried about the piglets. "Come on," she told Lexi as she threw down her bike and ran towards the paddock. "Let's go and check."

And *phew!* There they were – Roxy and Rosie snoozing inside the stable, snoring loudly.

* * *

"Benji, stay!" Lexi called.

It was two in the afternoon and she and

Lily were out in the main paddock, teaching Oliver's puppy some basic doggie rules.

Lily stayed with Benji while Lexi and Alfie walked ten paces across the field. "Benji, come!" Lexi called. She held up a small tasty reward.

Yip!

Lily let Benji go and watched him dart towards Lexi.

"Good boy!" Lexi told him as she patted him and gave him the treat.

"I hope those treats are non-fattening!" Matt called across the field as he brought a bowl of table scraps for the piglets.

"Totally!" Lily and Lexi called back.

"Give these to Roxy and Rosie when they wake up," he told the girls.

They didn't have to wait long. In fact, Matt wasn't back inside the house before the piglets were out of their stable and trotting eagerly towards the bowl.

"I swear they can smell food in their sleep!" Lexi laughed.

A beep from Lily's phone told her that she had a message. "It's from Emma and Charlie," she told Lexi as she began to read.

"Fetch!" Lexi told Benji and Alfie. She picked up a stick and threw it. "What's it say?" she asked Lily.

The dogs raced for the stick. Alfie got there first. He picked it up and ran back with Benji hard on his heels.

" 'Back in time for tea!' " Lily replied with a sigh.

"I know," Lexi agreed as she gazed at Roxy and Rosie happily munching sandwich crusts. "In a few more hours it'll be time to say goodbye."

Chapter Eight

"Yeah, we're really sad that you have to leave Muddy Paws," Lexi told Rosie. She went up to her in the pig run carrying a bucket of soapy water and a scrubbing brush. "But Lily and me will still come and visit you at Lane's End."

"You see this?" Lily said to Roxy. She too was carrying a brush and a bucket. They were girls on a mission. "We want to clean you up and make you all nice and pretty, ready to go home!"

"*Oink! Oink!*" The piglets raced up to

the girls, only to find that there was no food in the buckets. Disappointed, they head-butted them and splashed water everywhere.

Sploosh! Sploosh! Lily and Lexi's jeans were soaked.

Outside the paddock gate, clever Benji and Alfie kept a safe distance.

"Listen to what Lily is telling you," Lexi scolded Rosie. "This is lovely warm water and we're going to wash away all that yucky mud!"

Rosie sniffed, oinked and ran away. When Lily put her bucket down, Roxy turned, aimed and kicked it clean over with her back feet.

"O-o-oh . . . dear!" Lily watched the sudsy water sink into the ground. At this rate they'd never get anywhere.

"Rosie, come here!" Lexi insisted. But she found that piglets weren't at all like puppies – they didn't do a thing you told them.

Lily picked up her empty bucket. "Maybe this wasn't a good idea," she sighed.

"But we can't hand them back looking like this," Lexi argued. Roxy and Rosie's white coats were dusty grey and there were dark splodges of dried mud on their backs and tummies that hadn't been there when they first arrived. "Emma and Charlie will think we haven't looked after them properly."

So the girls set off down the run, dead set on cornering the piglets and giving them a good scrub.

"What have you got in your pockets?" Lily asked Lexi, who pulled out a small green apple. "Anything else?"

"No. How about you?"

"Just half a banana," Lily replied. She held it up in the air. "Here, pig, pig, pig!"

"Here, pig!" Lexi echoed.

But Rosie and Roxy wrinkled their snouts, flapped their floppy ears and kept on running until they came to the wire fence.

"Stop!" Lexi and Lily yelled. If the piglets crashed into the electrified tape they were in for a shock.

No brakes! Roxy and Rosie barged straight through the tape. They tore up two of the plastic poles that the girls had planted deep into the ground and then charged on.

"No!" Lily gasped. "What happened?"

No electricity was what happened – just plain, flimsy tapes and upturned fence posts trampled into the grass.

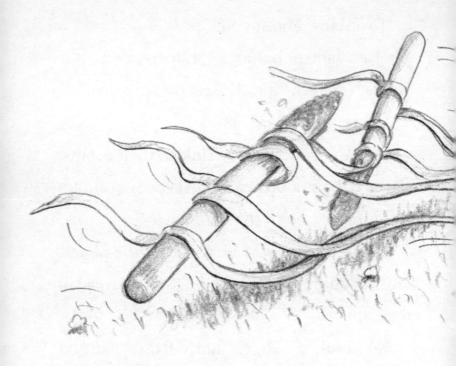

And the piglets were racing on across the paddock, straight for the rabbit warren by the hawthorn hedge.

"The switch!" Lexi realized. She thought back to what she'd done earlier that day.

"H-e-n-s!" she'd whispered in Lily's ear, trying to persuade her to leave the piglets for a while and cycle with her to Lane's End.

Then she'd dashed to the stable and flicked the switch to turn off the CD player. But she must have turned off the electric fence as well! Big, big mistake! "No!" she groaned.

"Yes!" Lily's heart sank.

Roxy and Rosie dug into the soft bank with their sharp trotters. They snorted and kicked up soil until they'd made a deep hole.

Then, with a final snort and a wiggle of their fat backsides, they squeezed through the hedge and vanished.

"Quick!" Lily reached the hedge first and went down on her hands and knees. "We have to follow them!"

"The hole's too small – we can't get through!" Frantically Lexi began to scrape at the soil with her bare hands.

Lily helped. Soon the hole was big enough to let them crawl under the hedge on to the cliff path. "Which way?" she cried.

Lexi pointed to trotter marks on the sandy track. "This way!"

Roxy and Rosie were out of sight but the girls were on the trail. Alfie and Benji had raced across the paddock to join them.

"Good dogs!" Lily said, out of breath from digging. "Find the piglets – fetch!"

Alfie understood. He sniffed at the ground and set off towards Lighthouse Cottages, closely followed by Benji.

"What do you bet they're headed back to Dentwood Hall?" Lexi said.

Nodding, Lily set off after the two excited dogs. "We've got food to tempt them back home when we find them. Let's hope it works."

"And fast!" Lexi gasped. She looked at her watch. "We've only got an hour at the most before Emma and Charlie arrive!"

* * *

Benji and Alfie followed the trotter trail along the cliff path. Lily and Lexi followed.

"I wish it wasn't so misty," Lexi grumbled.

"Actually it's getting worse." Lily looked down at the beach then out to sea. The tide was coming in and bringing more white mist with it.

"Good boys!" Lexi told the dogs as they stopped to sniff at the gate of Dentwood Hall. "What did I tell you?" she said to Lily. "Roxy and Rosie broke into Harry's garden, just like yesterday."

No sooner said than the gate flew open and Harry stepped out on to the track with a football under his arm. "I thought I heard voices," he said.

"Harry – Roxy and Rosie – where did they go?" Lily gasped.

As Alfie and Benji sniffed then ran back on to the path and took up a fresh trail, Harry shrugged his shoulders. "What are you talking about? I've been playing football on the lawn and I haven't seen any sign of the pesky piglets."

Lily and Lexi groaned.

"OK, Harry, we were wrong," Lily told him. "Can't stop to explain – sorry!"

Hurriedly the girls followed the dogs.

"Want any help?" Harry called after them.

"No thanks," Lexi said then stopped and turned. "Actually yes. Have you got a CD player handy?"

"A CD player?" He echoed the odd question.

"Yeah, you know. If you've got one, can you fetch it for us?"

Harry nodded. "Where will you be? How will I find you?"

"Just follow the trail!" Lexi cried as she ran to catch up with Lily, Alfie and Benji.

* * *

"Whoa, stop!" Lily told Lexi.

The trotter trail had come to an end by

the wooden steps down to the beach and Alfie and Benji were sniffing around in circles.

"Oh no – where did they go?" Lexi moaned. The mist was so thick she could only see fifteen metres ahead.

Sharp-eyed Lily searched for more tracks. "Maybe down the steps," she decided.

Alfie and Benji agreed. Tails in the air and noses to the ground, they veered off the track and on to the wooden steps, where they disappeared in the mist.

Lexi nodded. "Let's go."

Lily set off and counted the steps. ". . . Eleven, twelve, thirteen . . ." Though they could hardly see where they were going, she knew there were twenty-three steps before they reached the sand. ". . . Twenty-one, twenty-two, twenty-three."

"That's it – we're on the beach," she called back to Lexi. She could just see Alfie and Benji ahead of her and Lexi behind.

"I'm here," Lexi told her, looming out of the mist. They could hear the waves breaking nearby but couldn't actually see them.

"This is not good." Lily shook her head. In a mist like this, anyone could get lost. "Here, Alfie! Here, Benji!"

Yip! Benji appeared first, with Alfie close on his heels.

"Thanks heavens!" Lexi breathed a sigh of relief. "Stay!" she told them.

The pups sat and gazed up at the girls as the thick mist swirled around them.

"What now?" Lexi asked Lily, who took the squished banana out of her pocket.

"Here, pig, pig, pig!" she cried.

"Here, pig!"

Lexi held up her green apple. "Here, pig!"

But there was oink, no snort, no fat white piglets racing for the treats.

Except for the roar of the waves there was silence.

Chapter Nine

"Here, pig, pig, pig!" Lexi and Lily cried.

The waves crashed and the pups stayed close to heel as the girls' voices were swallowed by the mist.

"It's no good – they're never going to come back in time!" There was fear in Lily's voice, knowing that the tide would soon cover the sand and wash against the foot of the cliffs.

"Why isn't the food working?" Lexi wanted to know. Normally the piglets came dashing up at the first little whiff of something to eat. "Lily, you don't think . . . ?"

"Think what? That Roxy and Rosie got washed away by the waves?" Lily shuddered. "Here, pig!" she called again.

"Or maybe they ran the other way, towards the cliffs," Lexi said. "Let's take a look."

"All stick together," Lily insisted. A wave broke and lapped around her feet, showing that the tide was up even higher. "Hold hands," she told Lexi. "Alfie and Benji – come!"

Stumbling through the mist towards the rocks, they heard a voice in the distance and stopped.

"Lexi, Lily – I brought the CD player. Where are you?" Harry called from the bottom of the steps.

"Over here!" Lexi answered. "We'll wait for you!"

"What's the point of that?" Lily wanted to know. To her it seemed that they were wasting precious time. "We don't even have a CD!"

"Yes, we do!" Lexi told her. She slipped a hand into her pocket and drew out a slim plastic case. " 'Lucky Us' by Up Front!"

It seemed they waited ages for Harry to reach them and hand over the player, but at last he appeared out of the mist.

"Any sign of the piglets?" he gasped.

"Not yet." Lily admitted that the food treat hadn't worked. "We think they're hiding under the cliff."

"*We hope!*" Lexi added. If not, it seemed likely that poor Roxy and Rosie had been washed out to sea.

Carefully, one step at a time, Lily led the way. "Here, pig!" she called.

"So put on the disc," Harry urged Lexi.

Her fingers were cold and she fumbled to slide it into the player.

"Now press Play!"

"'We're so lucky – lucky, lucky, lucky!'" Jude, Luke, Sam and Ryan sang.

Whoosh! Another wave broke and crashed just behind them.

"Louder!" Lily told Lexi.

Lexi turned up the volume.

"'To be with you / Knowing you'll be true!'"

Together they strained to see through the mist, hoping and praying that they would see the runaway Old Spots.

"Oink!"

"Did you hear that?" Lily gasped. It was faint but she was sure she wasn't mistaken.

"Louder!" she begged.

"It won't go any higher," Lexi told her.

" '*Lucky, lucky, lucky – ooooooh!*' "

"*Oink! Oink!*" Not so faint this time.

Lily, Lexi, Harry, Alfie and Benji followed the direction of the piggy voices. They stepped through rock pools, sliding and splashing as they went.

"Here, pig!" Lily cried.

And there, at last – coming out from under a rocky ledge, ears flopping, trotters wading through water – were Roxy and Rosie!

They slipped and they slid, they sank up to their fat white bellies in seawater and seaweed, but they kept on coming.

"Thank you, Harry!" Lexi cried. She felt tears of relief well up as she dropped to her knees and held out the apple.

"Thank you, Up Front!" Lily peeled the remains of the banana.

"'*To be with you/Knowing you'll be tru-u-u-e!*'"

The piglets came out from under the cliff where they'd been hiding from the waves. They stretched out and sniffed, snuffled and snorted. Slowly, slowly, they came, and the moment they sank their teeth into the fruit,

Lily and Lexi grabbed them.

"Good job!" Harry cried. He knew they
had to get off the beach before the tide cut
them off.

"We'll follow you," Lexi told him. She
had her arms around Rosie's belly and Alfie
stuck close at heel. "Keep an eye on Benji!"
she called back to Lily.

Roxy squirmed in Lily's arms but she held

her tight. "Benji, come!" she told the little puppy, who trotted obediently behind.

Now the waves lapped around their feet, swirling into the rock pools and right up to the cliff face. They had to paddle towards the steps, praying that Harry would find the way.

"Quick – follow me!" he said, his voice shaking as the water grew deeper. "I'm at the steps. Come this way!"

First Lexi joined him, with Rosie and Alfie. Then Lily, Roxy and Benji arrived. Benji was soaked in salt water, dripping and bedraggled. But he wagged his tail and shook himself dry as he brought up the rear.

"Is everyone safe?" Lexi checked before she followed Harry up the steps to the cliff path.

"Yes, we all made it!" Lily sighed. And

tears of relief fell as she carried Roxy up
twenty-three steps to safety.

Chapter
Ten

Lexi and Lily carried Rosie and Roxy all the way home – up the steps from the beach and along the cliff path, only stopping to say goodbye to Harry at the gate to Dentwood Hall.

"By the way, my friend Dominic said yes to Eric the baby guinea pig," Harry told them as the Hall peacocks came running across the lawn.

"*E-e-elp!*" they cried.

"Coolio," Lily told him. "We'll tell Jon and Sam Simons the good news."

"See you soon, Harry," Lexi grinned as Rosie squirmed and wriggled in her arms.

The girls struggled on towards Sea View, letting Alfie and Benji run ahead until they saw the house through the mist. Lily's dad was waiting for them at the door.

"So it's not just head-banging heavy metal music that Roxy and Rosie like," Matt commented as he listened to the story of the piglets' narrow escape. He handed out towels then lined up the girls' wet boots by the side of the Aga.

"It turns out that what Emma said really is true," Lily explained as she dried Roxy with one of the towels. "They do love heavy metal. But they also like rap, opera, rock and pop – *any* kind of music!"

"And they really did come out from the rocks when they heard Up Front?" Matt

shook his head and smiled.

"*'Lucky, lucky, lucky!'*" Lexi sang as she dried Rosie.

"They just couldn't resist," Lily told her dad. "We'd tried tempting them with food, but it was Luke's music that did it."

"Well, I'm glad it all ended well," Matt told them. He looked out of the window to see Emma and Charlie Golding pull up in the café car park. "And just in time too!"

Hearing the bang and pop of the old Volvo exhaust, Lexi and Lily hurriedly wrapped the piglets in the towels and picked them up.

Roxy oinked and wriggled, Rosie snorted and squirmed as the girls carried them outside.

Emma was first out of the car. "What a terrible end to the journey," she sighed when she saw Lily and Lexi. "So much mist coming off the sea."

"Sorry if we're a little bit late," Charlie told them after he'd got the pet carrier out of the back of the estate car.

"No problem," the girls replied.

"Were the hens OK?" Emma asked Lily, who nodded.

"And the sheep." Lily told her that everyone at Lane's End was fine.

"And I hope these two little rascals didn't cause you too much trouble," Emma went on.

Lily unwrapped Roxy's towel and handed her over to Charlie. She chose her words carefully. "Actually, they were quite... lively!"

"As in, they ran away *twice*!" Lexi almost dropped Rosie as she handed her over to Emma. "But it was OK – Alfie and Benji helped us pick up the trail and our friend, Harry Finch, joined in the search."

"Naughty little pigs!" Emma scolded, catching hold of Rosie and popping her straight into the carrier. "Why couldn't you be good, just for once?"

"*Oink!*" Rosie replied, jumping straight

out again and skedaddling towards the café.
Cake, biscuits, scones!

Alfie and Benji cut her off before she reached the door. They herded her back towards the house.

"Great team effort!" Matt told the dogs as the Goldings got a firm hold of their piglets.

"In you go!" Charlie told Roxy. This time, he and Emma popped the piglets into the carrier at the same time.

"*Oink, oink!*" they said as Emma quickly closed the grille.

Lily and Lexi sighed. "Bye, Roxy! Bye, Rosie!"

"*Oink – snort – snuffle!*"

"We loved having them," Lily told Emma and Charlie. "They can come to Muddy Paws any time they like."

"We can't thank you enough for stepping in at the last minute," Charlie told Lexi and Lily as Emma put the pet carrier back into the Volvo.

The piglets peered out through the grille, shaking their heads and waggling their ears.

"So cute!" Lily and Lexi murmured.

Charlie closed the car door. "And you can come to Lane's End and see them any time you like," he invited.

The girls smiled and nodded. They waved

as the old car rattled and scraped its way out on to the road.

"What next for Muddy Paws?" Matt asked in the flat, empty moments that followed.

Lexi and Lily took deep breaths.

"Let's make a list," Lily suggested, counting items on her fingers. "One – tell the Simons twins the good news about Eric. Two – call Will Jonson to check up on Robbie the rabbit."

"Three – update the Muddy Paws website with more facts about Gloucester Old Spots," Lexi continued. "Four – put up a picture of Caspar the lost kitten."

"But before that it's time for tea," Matt reminded them. "Lily, why not pop over to the café and ask your mum if there are any spare cream cakes we could have?"

Lexi liked the sound of that. "Wait for me

– I'll come too," she said.

So the girls ran across the lawn into the tea shop, looking for Jo.

"She's not here," Lexi frowned. In fact, the café looked closed for the day.

"She's probably in the gift shop," Lily decided. "Mum?" she called as she opened the connecting door.

Sure enough, Jo was behind her counter, counting up the day's takings. But she'd stopped what she was doing and was listening instead. "Ssshhh!" she warned.

Lily paused just inside the shop. "Why – what is it?"

"*Miaow!*" Lexi and Lily heard a faint cry. "*Mia-o-o-ow!*"

"Over there!" Jo pointed towards a basket full of dog toys in the corner of the shop.

"*Miaow!*" The girls held their breaths and tiptoed towards the sound.

"Close the door," Lexi whispered to Lily. "Help me move the basket."

Slowly and gently they slid the basket to one side.

"*Miaow!*" A tiny grey cat stared up at them with big green eyes.

"Caspar!" Lexi and Lily knew at once who'd wandered by chance into the Sea View gift shop. It was June Amos's missing kitten.

"Here, kitty, kitty, kitty!" Lexi called softly and stooped to pick up what to her was the fluffiest, cutest kitten in the world.

Lily took out her phone. "Hello, is that Mrs Amos? It's Lily from Muddy Paws here."

Lexi snuggled the lost kitten under her

chin and heard him purr. She grinned at Lily.

"About Caspar," Lily told the worried owner. "Well, we've got some very good news . . . !"

Turn the page
for a sneak preview
of the next book . . .

Saving
Snowdrop

Turn the page
for a sneak preview
of the next book . . .

When Mrs Taylor came into the room, they sat down at their table.

"Only one day to go until the school trip!" Lexi whispered to Tom Starling. In her head she happily pictured fluffy yellow chicks, piglets with curly tails and of course the three newborn lambs.

He frowned and looked glum. "Yeah, and guess what?"

"What?" Lily asked. Why wasn't Tom happy about the class visit to his farm?

"Today Mrs Taylor is going to make me

stand up and give a talk," he muttered as the teacher called out names from the register.

"A talk about your farm?" Lexi hissed at Tom.

He shuffled in his seat. "Yeah – she wants me to tell people about the lambs."

"For our Moor Top Farm project?" Lily asked.

He nodded. "I have to say how they're born and all that stuff."

Lily and Lexi could see this wouldn't be easy for Tom. The farmer's son was the quiet, thoughtful type who liked to sit at the back of the class. He wasn't exactly unfriendly – just shy.

As the time for his talk drew near, they watched him take a sheet of paper out of his bag and hold it between trembling hands.

"Stand up, Tom," Mrs Taylor instructed

kindly. "Speak in a nice, clear voice."

His face turned deep red as he started to read. "'How Lambs Are Born'," he began. "'Most lambs are born between February and April. We bring the pregnant ewes into a field near the farmyard.'"

Lily took notes. She wanted to remember every single thing he told them.

"'One hour before the ewe gives birth, she leaves the flock and looks for a quiet corner. The lamb is born head first. Once the head and shoulders come out, the rest is very quick. The head is covered in a slimy coating called the mucus membrane.'"

"Yuck!" Emma muttered under her breath.

"Sshh!" Lexi warned.

"'The mother licks the lamb's face clean. After twenty minutes the lamb begins to suck.'" As Tom came to the end of his talk, he slowed down and looked up from his paper. "Is that OK, Miss? I took pictures of our first three lambs. Do you want to see them?"

"Yes please, Tom," Mrs Taylor said. "Give them to me at playtime and I'll stick them on the notice-board." She smiled at him. "Well done and thank you very much. Now we can all look forward to meeting the lambs at Moor Top Farm in person, remembering everything you've told us."

* * *

The whole school went out to play, then as soon as playtime was finished, Lily and Lexi rushed back into the classroom and looked eagerly at Tom's photos. Each picture showed a woolly lamb with a black face and black, wobbly legs.

"What are they called?" they wanted to know.

Tom shrugged. "We get so many lambs we don't give them names."

"But *we* can," Lexi decided. "We could have a class vote. Let's ask Mrs Taylor."

"Good idea," the teacher said when Lily and Lexi suggested it to her. "Everyone think of a name, write it down, fold up your piece of paper and pop it into my felt-tip pen box. We'll pick out three and they'll be the names we'll give to Tom's lambs."

"Mary." Lily wrote carefully on her scrap of paper. Just like the girl in the nursery rhyme. "'Mary had a little lamb . . .'"

Lexi thought hard then wrote down her suggestion. "Snowdrop." She crossed her fingers as she dropped her paper into the box.

After the whole class had finished, Mrs Taylor asked Tom to pick out the first piece of paper.

"Will you read it, Miss?" he asked shyly.

"'Amy'," the teacher announced, pinning the name next to the first picture. "Next?"

"Mary," Lily muttered, hoping that her name would come out of the box.

"'. . . Skippy'," Mrs Taylor announced, pinning up the second choice.

Lily felt a little disappointed.

"Snowdrop." Lexi kept her fingers crossed and silently mouthed her chosen name.

"'. . . Snowdrop'," Mrs Taylor said.

"Yes!" Lexi grinned. Her suggestion had been picked out of the box. How lucky was that!

"That's a good name," Lily admitted as they went back to their seats. Really – Snowdrop was a great name for a lamb, and so were Amy and Skippy. Yes, everything was cool and the best thing was – tomorrow was almost here!

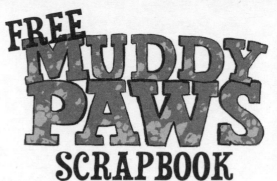

FREE MUDDY PAWS SCRAPBOOK

Find out what happens to Lexi and Lily in *Saving Snowdrop* – another Muddy Paws adventure – and receive a FREE Muddy Paws scrapbook!
The scrapbook is the ideal place for you to put pictures of all your favourite animals and pets. Plus there are activities perfect for all Muddy Paws fans!

To receive your Muddy Paws scrapbook, you need to collect two tokens. One is below and you'll find other tokens in the rest of the Muddy Paws series. Then simply fill in the form on this page and send it to us with both tokens and we'll send you your FREE Muddy Paws scrapbook!

Send one completed form and two tokens to: The Muddy Paws Scrapbook Offer,
e Marketing Department, Hachette Children's Books, 338 Euston Road, London, NW1 3BH

Closing date: 30 April 2014

TERMS AND CONDITIONS
(1) Open to UK and Republic of Ireland residents only (2) You must provide the email address of a parent or guardian for your entry
to be valid (3) Photocopied tokens are not accepted (4) The form must be completed fully for your entry to be valid (5) Scrapbooks are
distributed on a first come, first served basis while stocks last (6) No part of the offer is exchangeable for cash or any other offer
7) Please allow 28 days for delivery (8) Your details will only be used for the purposes of fulfilling this offer and, if you choose [see tick box below], to receive email newsletters about other great Hachette Children's books, and will never be shared with any third party.

✂

ease complete using capital letters (UK Residents Only)

ONE TOKEN

RST NAME:

RNAME:

TE OF BIRTH: DD MM YYYY

DRESS LINE 1:

DRESS LINE 2:

DRESS LINE 3:

STCODE:

RENT OR GUARDIAN'S EMAIL:

I'm happy to receive email newsletters and information about other great
Hachette Children's books (I can unsubscribe at any time).

www.hachettechildrens.co.uk